MONSTER IN THE MANGROVES

By Reese Ev~~erett~~

Illustrated by Sal~~~~

Rourke
Educational Media
rourkeeducationalmedia.com

www.rourkeeducationalmedia.com

Edited by: Keli Sipperley
Cover layout by: Renee Brady
Interior layout by: Rhea Magaro
Cover and Interior Illustrations by: Sally Garland

Library of Congress PCN Data

Monster in the Mangroves / Reese Everett
(Rourke's Beginning Chapter Books)
ISBN (hard cover)(alk. paper) 978-1-63430-377-4
ISBN (soft cover) 978-1-63430-477-1
ISBN (e-Book) 978-1-63430-573-0
Library of Congress Control Number: 2015933734

Dear Parents and Teachers:

Realistic fiction is ideal for readers transitioning from picture books to chapter books. In Rourke's Beginning Chapter Books, young readers will meet characters that are just like them. They will be drawn in by the familiar settings of school and home and the familiar themes of sports, friendship, feelings, and family. Young readers will relate to the characters as they experience the ups and downs of growing up. At this level, making connections with characters is key to developing reading comprehension.

Rourke's Beginning Chapter Books offer simple narratives organized into short chapters with some illustrations to support transitional readers. The short, simple sentences help readers build the needed stamina to conquer longer chapter books.

Whether young readers are reading the books independently or you are reading with them, engaging with them after they have read the book is still important. We've included several activities at the end of each book to make this both fun and educational.

By exposing young readers to beginning chapter books, you are setting them up to succeed in reading!

Enjoy,
Rourke Educational Media

Table of Contents

CHAPTER 1
LET ME EXPLAIN

I almost stepped on a dinosaur today. It got me in some trouble. Mostly because I didn't follow Mom's STAY WITH YOUR SISTER AND I MEAN IT rule. The thing is, I tried, but my tooth fell out in the middle of a walking tree forest. Then we saw this ginormous eyeball! There was some screaming. Tyler did most of it. I yelled a little, too. And then –

Well, maybe I should start at the beginning.

CHAPTER 2
SATURDAY TRASHED

"Lawrence, come down here," Mom yelled. I was in my room preparing to spend the day doing my favorite thing: nothing. It was Saturday. I liked to call it Sit All Day. I had six episodes of *Gruesome Goblin Guys* to watch and a new zombie video game to play.

"Coming!" I yelled back. I waited a few minutes. I hoped she would forget.

"LAWRENCE!"

She didn't.

I found her in the kitchen. It was full of smells. Most of them were bad. "What is that?" I asked, holding my nose.

"I made breakfast, but then I got a call from the hospital and I forgot about it," Mom said, waving her hand around like she was trying to do a magic spell to get rid of the odor. It wasn't working. "I have to do an emergency surgery today. You'll have to go with Rene to volunteer at the beach cleanup."

"What? Why? I can stay here, I'm fine! I've got things to do!" I said. "Important things," I added.

"Lawrence, you are eight years old, you're not staying home alone," she said. "Go get dressed, she can't be late. They're taking a boat somewhere or something." She turned back toward the oven disaster.

"But, but, I," I started to argue. Then I turned around and walked out, because I knew Saturday Sit All Day was shot.

I also knew my sister would drag me to the beach in my pajamas if she had to, so I hurried up and got dressed.

My sister is a senior in high school. That means she thinks she knows everything. She also wants to be a marine biologist, so she volunteers for a bunch of stuff. She'd been talking about today's beach cleanup at dinner all week. The team leader, Nate, was "SO smart and talented," she said. I heard her tell Mom he was really cute, too. Barf.

Rene opened my door without knocking and said, "You ready, hairy Larry?" I threw a pillow at her because I hate when she calls me that. She just laughed and said, "Let's go, kiddo."

I hate when she calls me that, too.

CHAPTER 3
SHARK SNACK

It took about 30 minutes to get to the boat dock. Rene kept telling me that I really better be on my best behavior and also not to talk too much.

"Do NOT embarrass me," she said. I didn't promise anything. I didn't want to go to the dumb beach cleanup, anyway. I didn't even like the beach. It was hot and the seagulls always tried to steal my snacks.

At the boat dock, a group of people gathered around a guy wearing a red bathing suit and a white tank top. He had a tattoo of an otter on his arm. It was pretty cool, actually.

"Hey, Rene," he said when he saw us. I made kissy noises at my sister.

"Shut it," she hissed at me. I made another kissy noise.

"Hey, Nate," Rene said, ignoring me. "This is my brother, Lawrence. He's really excited to help out today, aren't you, kiddo?" She peered over the top of her sunglasses at me. The look in her eyes said, "Say yes, or else."

"Yep," I said.

"Great," Nate said. "I was just about to go over a few things before we get on the boat."

Nate told us what we should pick up when we got started: any non-biodegradable trash, like bottles and Styrofoam containers. "

Don't pick the weeds and shake all the sand off the debris before it goes in the trash buckets," he said. "The sand and weeds are important to the island's ecosystem."

"Why is this island so trashy, anyway?" I asked Rene as we got on the boat.

"It isn't usually," Rene said. "That storm we had a few weeks ago picked up a lot of debris from the mainland and the docked boats. A good amount of it washed up on the island and got tangled in the mangroves."

"What are mangroves?" I asked. A red-haired boy plopped down on the seat next to me and flipped through a tattered book.

"These are mangroves," he said, pointing to a picture on the page. "They're trees that grow in saltwater. There are several species. Red mangroves are called walking trees because of their funny roots." He closed the book and looked up at me. "I'm Tyler." He reached out to shake my hand. His left pinky finger was missing.

"Cool. Where's your finger?" I asked, shaking his hand very grownup-like.

"A shark ate it," he said.

"Oh, Tyler," a short woman wearing a captain's hat said. She smiled and shook her head. Then she sat down behind the wheel and revved up the boat's engine.

"That's my mom," Tyler said. "A shark really did eat it, so don't put your hands in the water," he whispered. Sweat trickled down his freckled nose. Sweat also ran down my back. I reached around and wiped it, then patted my sister's leg.

"Ew!" she said.

Tyler laughed. I gave him a thumbs up.

CHAPTER 4
ROBOT TACOS
AND TREASURE MAPS

The boat ride was fast and a little loud. It was hard to hear anything above the wind and the motor. I noticed a girl sitting across from us reading *Robot Tacos Take over Tokyo*. The wind kept blowing her long blonde hair into her eyes and mouth. It made me glad my hair was short.

When we got to the island, Tyler's Mom tied the boat to the dock. Nate told us to grab one of the buckets piled up at the front of the boat. He grabbed a plastic bin full of supplies and headed off the boat first.

Tyler and I grabbed buckets and rushed after him.

"Wait up, Lawrence," Rene said. "Mom won't let me go to prom if I lose you on an island."

I stopped walking. UMP! Someone behind me bumped hard into my back.

"Sorry," the Robot Tacos reader girl said, looking up from her book. "I didn't see you stop."

I laughed. "It's okay. That's my favorite book."

She chattered nonstop as we joined the other volunteers gathered around Nate. "I've read all the Robot Tacos books! *Robot Tacos Plunder Paris* is my favorite! I love when they take over the museum and make all the paintings come to life!"

"How do tacos make things come to life?" Tyler asked.

"Hot pepper powers," I said.

He looked at me. Then he looked at reader girl. "You guys are weird."

She ignored him. "I'm Bella," she said to me.

"Lawrence," I said. "And that's Tyler. What are you doing here anyway?"

"My Dad had to work today so I had to tag along with my brother," Bella said.

"Me too. I had the best day ever planned and now I'm stuck picking up garbage with my sister," I said.

Nate was giving instructions. Rene leaned over and told me to shush. Bella giggled.

"Everyone needs to grab some gloves and a shovel. Don't pick up anything with your bare hands. Pay attention to the areas under the mangroves. Trash gets tangled in the roots. You can come back here and dump your buckets into this bin when they get full." He pointed to a black container marked TRASH.

"You need to stay with me," Rene said to me.

"Argh, I'm not a baby, I can go with Tyler and Bella," I said.

"My mom is staying on the boat so I am supposed to tag along with –"

"Gear up, Bella and Tyler," Nate interrupted. "You're with me."

I saw my sister's eyes get wide for a second. Then she quickly made her face look less silly. I snickered. She poked me in the ribs.

"The kids want to stick together," Rene said. I could tell she was trying to be cool. "May we join your crew?"

"Sure," Nate said. He smiled at my sister. My sister smiled back at him, then looked down at her feet. Tyler and I looked at each other and made gagging noises. We cracked up. Bella laughed, too.

"Let's go, goofballs," Nate said. He and Rene started toward a section of the beach no one was covering yet. We walked slowly behind them, looking for stuff to pick up.

"Check this out!" Bella said. She kneeled down next to a blob of clear gunk on the sand.

"It's a jellyfish," Tyler said. "Don't touch it, it could still sting you. That's how I lost my pinky."

"I thought you said a shark ate it," I said.

"A jellyfish stung it, then the shark ate it," he said. His face looked serious.

"That is not true," Bella said.

"It could be," he said.

Nate and Rene were far ahead of us now. I was not in a hurry to catch up to them. We kept walking. I picked up a crumpled can and a few bottle caps. Bella picked up a glass bottle and a plastic sandwich bag. Tyler found a piece of paper half buried in the sand. It had handwriting and sketches on it but it had gotten wet so the ink was blurry.

"Maybe it's a treasure map," Bella said.

I hoped so. That would make this volunteering stuff much more interesting.

"We should keep it, just in case," I said. Tyler folded it carefully and put it in his pocket.

CHAPTER 5
WALKING TREES

I could still see Rene and Nate ahead of us. They were bent down looking at something in the sand. I was curious, but not enough to catch up to them. I'd had enough of her calling me "kiddo" for one day. Plus, I didn't want to listen to their boring talk.

Bella, Tyler, and I decided to head toward the mangroves. "That's where all the trash is, anyway," I said.

We found a lot of junk floating around in the shallow water surrounding the trees. We filled my bucket and Bella's in just a couple minutes. As we walked farther into the mangrove forest, branches fanned out over us, blocking the sun. It felt like we were in a tunnel. A tunnel made of creepy trees with a million legs.

"These trees look like they want to eat us," I said.

"Don't be a scaredy pants," Bella said. "They're just trees." She wiped some sweat off of her forehead. I thought she might wipe it on me or Tyler but she wiped it on her shorts instead.

"I'm not scared. I just don't want to be eaten," I said.

Bella looked at me funny. "Open your mouth," she said.

"Why?" I said, then clamped my mouth shut tight. I didn't want her putting anything gross in there.

"I saw something, just open it."

I opened it and said *AHHH* like at the doctor's office. "There's nothing in there, see?"

"Didn't you have your front tooth a minute ago?" she asked.

I felt my teeth with my tongue. "My tooth finally came out," I said. "YES!" I jumped up and pumped my fist and scraped my head on a branch. But I didn't care. "Tooth Fairy, CHA-CHING!"

"I'm getting a new bike, I'm getting a new bike, woot woot, I'm getting a – "

I stopped my celebration dance when it hit me: I didn't have any idea where my tooth was. Without it, there would be no Tooth Fairy money. My stomach felt like I'd been punched in the gut.

"Guys, no one move. This is a real emergency," I said. "When was the last time you saw me with that tooth in my mouth?"

"I wasn't staring at your mouth. That would be weird," Tyler said.

"I need that thing," I said, sort of whiney. "The Tooth Fairy would've brought me the last $2 I need for my new bike."

"Well, that bites," Tyler said.

Bella said she knew I had it when we first got to the mangroves. "I saw it when you told that elephant poop joke," she said.

"HA HA! That was such a good one!" Tyler laughed.

"Maybe we'll find it while we're picking up the rest of this junk?" Bella said, pointing around to some cans and wrappers floating between the roots.

I ran my tongue over the empty spot in my mouth. I looked around all the places we'd been since the poop joke. That tooth could be anywhere.

"Let's just keep an eye out for it," I said. "We have to fill Tyler's bucket anyway."

I bent over to pick up an old ball wedged between some roots. It felt mushy in my hand. And when I turned it over to look at it, it looked back at me.

CHAPTER 6
MONSTER!

"AHHHHHHH!" I screamed and dropped the giant eyeball. It landed by my feet. Water splashed up on the rain boots Rene made me wear. *Water and eyeball gook,* I thought.

"What is that?" Tyler shrieked. He jumped up and down and shook his arms like he had the heeby jeebies.

Bella crouched down to get a closer look. She poked it with her finger. I shuddered.

"It's definitely an eyeball," she said. She did not scream or do the heeby jeeby dance. She just stood up and looked around. Then she said something horrible.

"I've never seen an eyeball this big. It looks like ... like ... a monster's eye. What if it's still alive?" She whispered the last part. But I heard her. Tyler heard her too.

"You mean what if there is a giant monster in the mangroves watching us with his one eye?" I said. We all looked around. There was nothing around. Nothing we could see, anyway. No one said anything. The eery quiet made my hairs stand up on my arms.

Then we heard shouting. *It's eating someone!* I thought.

"Run!" Tyler said.

We took off into the trees, away from the yelling. We jumped and tripped over mangrove roots. Tyler's shirt snagged on a branch. He ripped it and kept running.

"Wait!" Bella called from behind us.

I stopped and turned toward her voice. "Hurry!" I yelled back.

I turned to run again. I raised my foot to leap over a giant rock.

Then the rock moved.

CHAPTER 7
DINO ROCK

I screamed. I was doing a lot of screaming. I fell sideways so I wouldn't step on it. I landed in a clump of roots. Tyler ran back toward me. Bella caught up to us. She was still carrying her bucket. Tyler and I had dropped ours on the run from the one-eyed beast.

"Whoa, cool!" Tyler said, pointing to the moving rock.

"Awesome!" Bella said. "I've never seen one up close before!"

"What is it?" I asked. I wasn't sure I wanted to know.

Bella laughed. "It's a sea turtle!"

"A loggerhead sea turtle," Tyler said. "They're an endangered species. I learned about them in my book." He crossed his arms and crouched down to get a closer look at the giant turtle.

I stood up to get a better look, too. The thing looked like it weighed about 200 pounds!

"These guys have been around for 200 million years," Tyler said. "My book calls them the last of the ancient reptiles. It's pretty much a dinosaur!"

"We should move away so it's not scared," Bella said. "It is probably trying to get back to the ocean."

"We should go back, too," I said. "My sister is going to be mad." We were so far into the trees I thought we might be near the opposite side of the island by now.

"But that's where the screaming came from," Tyler said. His face looked pale. It made the freckles on his cheeks seem darker. "If the monster is still looking for its eye, it's back that way, too."

"Not exactly," Bella said. She pointed to her bucket.

"You brought it with you?" Tyler put his hands over his face. "Now we're all gonna be monster meat!"

"No, we're not," I said. "I cannot be monster meat. I have a bike to buy tomorrow." Except I still hadn't found my tooth. I was hoping the Tooth Fairy would understand if I wrote her – him? – a note.

"Guys, look," Bella pointed to the sea turtle. It was trying to move but it couldn't. Its foot was caught on something.

We were leaning over trying to get a better look when we heard the sound of footsteps crashing toward us.

"Oh, no," Tyler said. "It's coming. And it wants its eye!"

CHAPTER 7
RELEASE THE BEAST

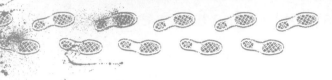

The footsteps were getting closer. "Should we run?" I asked.

"We can't leave the turtle stuck here," Bella said. "We have to cut it loose somehow."

"Yeah, the one-eye monster may eat it," Tyler said. "Like it did my pinky." He wiggled his hand at us and shuddered.

"It did not eat your pinky," I said.

"It could have," Tyler said.

The sloshing footsteps got closer and stopped. Gulp.

"Lawrence. Joseph. Ramsey." I heard my sister's voice say. It sounded scarier than any monster could. Rene and Nate appeared, holding their buckets, plus mine and Tyler's.

"What in the world were you thinking wandering off? We've been looking for you everywhere. Couldn't you hear us yelling?" Rene looked a little like a monster at the moment, too. Her hair was wild and her eyes were squinty and mad-looking. It sort of made me want to laugh. But I didn't. I just snorted a little.

"We were cleaning up the mangroves," I said. "And then my tooth fell out –"

Tyler cut me off. "And then there was a monster eye and we heard yelling so we ran and Lawrence stepped on a dinosaur but it's not really a dinosaur –"

"It's a sea turtle and it's stuck," Bella said, pointing at the creature behind us.

Rene and Nate came over to get a closer look.

"Yikes, she's really tangled up in something," Nate said. "It's a good thing you found her. Let's get her out of this mess." He stood and hugged Bella. Then he gave me and Tyler fist bumps.

Rene mouthed some words at me when no one was looking. I think they were "You're still in trouble," or maybe they were "Poor little brother." I kept my fingers crossed it was the second one.

Nate sat down next to the giant turtle and talked quietly to it. "You're gonna be okay, girl, we'll help you," he said as he carefully cut away at the thick plastic around her back flipper.

We cheered when Nate cut away the last piece. The turtle still didn't move, though.

"Do you think she's okay?" Bella asked.

"I think so," Nate said. He stood up and put his pocketknife back in his pocket. "She'll make her way back to the water once we're out of the way. She's probably a bit scared of us."

"You guys ready to head back?" Rene asked.

"Yes," Tyler said, grabbing his bucket. "Let's get out of here before the monster sniffs out his eye." He looked at Bella's bucket and did the heeby jeeby dance.

"What are you talking about?" Rene said. Bella pulled the softball-size eyeball from the bucket. She turned it so that it stared at us. Rene jumped and screamed. "What IS that?"

"Whoa," Nate said. "That is a monster eye!"

CHAPTER 9
EYE SEE YOU

We headed back toward the boats, picking up every piece of trash we saw on the way. After seeing what the trash did to that poor turtle, I didn't want to leave a single piece behind. We took the giant eyeball with us, too. Nate said Tyler's mom might know what kind of animal it came from. Tyler said he already knew.

"Sea monster," he said. "Case closed. Now can we hurry and get out of here?"

"I still want to find my tooth," I said. "Keep an eye out, will you?"

Bella pulled the eye from the bucket. She made it look all around.

"Very funny," I said. Then I keeled over laughing because actually it was a riot. Everyone else laughed, too.

Back at the boat, the other volunteers were dumping their buckets into the bin then heading back out to collect more trash. We dumped ours, too, then climbed aboard the boat, where we found Tyler's mom flipping through a tattered notebook and muttering to herself. "Where in the world is that thing? I know it was in here. Ugh."

She looked up when Bella sat the bucket down next to her. "Oh, hey guys! How's the cleanup going? Sorry I couldn't lend a hand today, big test Monday. Trying to study but I — " she glanced down at the bucket. "WHOA! Cool!" She reached in and pulled the monster eye out. Then she put it up close to her face, like she was gonna have a staring contest with it.

"Do you know what this is?" she asked. She turned the eye toward us and waved it around. Tyler shuddered.

Nate laughed. "We were hoping you did," he said.

"It's a swordfish eye," she said. "Probably from a guy that was about 1,000 pounds. A fisherman probably caught the beast and dumped the parts. Was likely a real beauty." She peered at the eyeball and shook her head. "Mind if I keep this for my specimen collection? My passengers love to see the weird stuff."

We agreed. Tyler groaned. "Great, now that thing will be staring at me the rest of my life," he said, shoving his hands in his pockets. Then he made a funny face and pulled out the paper we'd found earlier. "Forgot this was in here," he said.

"What is it?" Rene asked. We all peered over Tyler's shoulder as he unfolded it.

"Some kind of treasure map or something," I said.

"WOOHOO!" Tyler's mom shouted. Then she snatched that thing right out of his hand!

CHAPTER 10
THIEF!

"MOM! Are you stealing our treasure map? What kind of mother ARE you?" Tyler glared at the boat captain as she shoved the paper into her notebook.

"What?" She looked back at us. We all must have had shocked faces because she laughed, then looked a little ashamed. "I'm sorry, I shouldn't have grabbed it like that. That was rude. I've just been looking for that paper all day. It's from my class notes for this test. The wind must've picked it up and sent it flying toward the beach when I wasn't looking."

"Oh," Tyler said. He looked disappointed. So did Bella. I was bummed, too. I really needed some treasure since I lost my stinkin' tooth.

"Maybe you'll find a real treasure map at next weekend's cleanup?" Nate said. He winked at us.

Spend another Saturday picking up trash instead of watching Gruesome Goblin Guys? I thought.

"We'll be going out to Monkey Island next time," Nate said.

I looked at Bella and Tyler. "We're in," we all said at the same time.

"Jinx," we all said. "Jinx again," we chorused. "Jinx again!"

Dear Miss (or Mister?) Tooth Fairy,

Let me first say that you are my favorite. Really. I'm your #1 fan. So I hope you will not be too disappointed that I do not actually have my tooth for you to take this time. See, I lost it when I was cleaning up the beach. Do you take shark teeth? I found one of those, so I'm leaving it here for you, just in case. It's way cooler than mine anyway. Tyler said it's from the shark that ate his pinky. I don't really know if that's true. But it could be.

Your pal,
Lawrence

Reflection

When Mom said I had to go with my sister to pick up trash at the beach, I was SO bummed. My Saturday was totally ruined! Or at least I thought it was. It ended up being the best day ever. I made awesome new friends and we saved an amazing sea turtle. That's the part I keep thinking about. Cleaning up doesn't just make things look prettier, it can save lives. Now Rene is stuck with me on cleanup days, because volunteering is way cool. I like the way helping out makes me feel, like I'm proud and happy and sort of exhausted all at once. Also I'm still hoping to find some treasure someday.

Discussion Questions

1. Why didn't Lawrence want to go with his sister to volunteer?

2. Was it wrong for the kids to wander away from Rene and Nate?

3. Why do you think Tyler makes up stories about his missing finger?

4. Have you ever found anything mysterious? What was it?

5. Do you think it is important to spend time volunteering? Why or why not?

Vocabulary

Make a matching memory game! Write each word below on an index card. Then write the definition of the words on another set of index cards. Shuffle them all up and lay them face down. When it's your turn, flip a card over. Then flip a second card over. If your cards are a match, you keep them. Whoever gets the most matches wins!

biodegradable
debris
endangered
flyer
hissed
mainland
opposite
shallow

Writing Prompt

We have lots of opportunities to support each other every day. Think about the ways you've helped people, animals, or the environment. Write about how doing something for others made you feel.

Q & A with Author Reese Everett

Have you ever volunteered for something?

I have! Sometimes I help out at a food bank, putting together boxes for families in need. Sometimes I volunteer to help at events that raise money for special causes. I've never done a beach cleanup, but writing this book made me want to! I spend a lot of time at the beach, so it's important to me that beaches are protected and cared for.

Where did you get the ideas for this story?

A few things inspired this story. I read about a giant eyeball that was found on a beach in Florida. Some people thought it could be from a strange sea monster. No one knew where it came from until scientists ran tests on it. They decided it came from a swordfish. I also have a friend who loves to play zombie games. The rest I dreamed up while running my favorite trail at a park near my house. If you need to think and be creative, getting outside can really do the trick.

Connections

You can help the environment by picking up trash when you see it. Whether you are at a beach, a park, a campground, or just in your own backyard, pitching in to help clean up the planet is always a great thing! Just make sure you keep safety in mind. Don't pick up glass or other sharp objects with your hands. If you're not sure, ask an adult to help you.

It is also important to only pick up items that shouldn't be there. Shake the sand off of the trash before you put it in the garbage. Don't pull weeds or take stones, sticks, or other natural objects. Take the trash, leave nature behind!

Websites to Visit

http://kidsoceanday.org

http://pbskids.org/zoom/activities/action/
    way04.html

http://kidshealth.org/kid/feeling/thought/
    volunteering.html

About the Author

Reese Everett is a
children's book author
from Tampa, Florida. She
loves her four kids, silly
adventures, and sunny
days at the beach. And
avocados. Her favorite
thing to see is people being kind and
helpful to others.

About the Illustrator

Sally Anne Garland was born in Hereford England and moved to the Highlands of Scotland at the age of three. She studied Illustration at Edinburgh College of Art before moving to Glasgow where she now lives with her partner and young son.